Ladybird  Readers

Willy and Harry

To access the audio and digital versions
of this book:

1 Go to **www.ladybirdeducation.co.uk**
2 Click "Unlock book"
3 Enter the code below

5LGj9KZtEq

Notes to teachers, parents, and carers

The **Ladybird Readers** Beginner level helps young language learners to become familiar with key conversational phrases in English. The language introduced has clear real-life applications, giving children the tools to hold their first conversations in English.

This book focuses on asking and responding to the question "Are we friends?" and provides practice of saying "happy" and "sad" in English. The pictures that accompany the text show a range of settings, which may be used to introduce one or two pieces of topic-based vocabulary, such as "walk" and "run", if the children are ready.

There are some activities to do in this book. They will help children practice these skills:

 Speaking    Listening*   Reading   Singing*

*To complete these activities, listen to the audio downloads available at www.ladybirdeducation.co.uk

Series Editor: Sorrel Pitts
Text adapted by Nicole Irving
Song lyrics by Wardour Studios

LADYBIRD BOOKS

UK | USA | Canada | Ireland | Australia
India | New Zealand | South Africa

Ladybird Books is part of the Penguin Random House group of companies
whose addresses can be found at global.penguinrandomhouse.com.
www.penguin.co.uk   www.puffin.co.uk   www.ladybird.co.uk

Penguin
Random House
UK

Text adapted from *Willy and Hugh* by Anthony Browne, first published by Julia MacRae, 1991
This Ladybird Readers edition published 2021
001

Text and illustrations copyright © A.E.T. Browne & Partners, 1991
The moral right of the original author and the original illustrator has been asserted

Printed in China
A CIP catalogue record for this book is available from the British Library

ISBN: 978-0-241-47552-2

All correspondence to:
Ladybird Books
Penguin Random House Children's
One Embassy Gardens, 8 Viaduct Gardens, London SW11 7BW

Willy and Harry

Based on *Willy and Hugh*
by Anthony Browne

"I am sad," Willy says.

"I want a friend."

"Are we friends?" Willy says.
"No!"

7

"I am sad," Willy says.

"I want a friend."

9

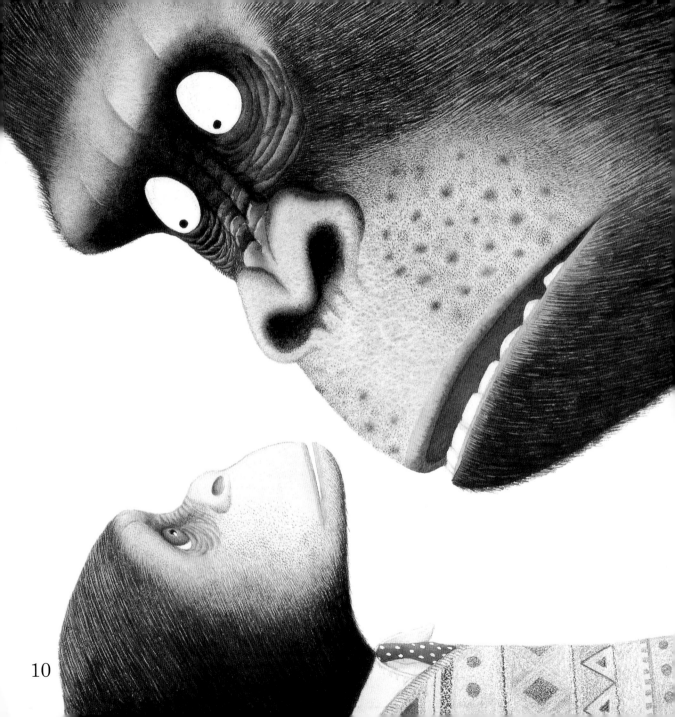

10

"I am sorry," Willy says.
"No! I am sorry," Harry says.

"Are we friends?" Willy says.

Willy is happy.
Harry is happy.

"We are friends," Harry says.

Your turn!

1 **Talk with a friend.**

I am sorry.

I am sorry!

Are we friends?

We are friends.

2 Listen and read. Match. 🎧 📖

1 Willy is sad.

2 Willy is happy.

3 Harry says,
"I am sorry."

4 Harry is happy.

3 Sing the song.

I want a friend. Are we friends?
No, no, no! We are not friends.
Willy, Willy, Willy says, "I am sorry!"
Harry, Harry, Harry says, "No, I am sorry!"

I want a friend. Are we friends?
Yes, yes, yes! We are friends!
Willy, Willy, Willy is happy, happy, happy.
Harry, Harry, Harry is happy, happy, happy.

I want a friend. Are we friends?
Yes, yes, yes! We are friends!
I want a friend. Are we friends?
Yes, yes, yes! We are friends!